SandCastle

Word Families Set 3

-ill as in grill

Kelly Doudna

Consulting Editor Monica Marx, M.A./Reading Specialist

ABDO Publishing Company

Published by SandCastle™, an imprint of ABDO Publishing Company, 4940 Viking Drive, Edina, Minnesota 55435.

Printed in the United States.

Credits
Edited by: Pam Price
Curriculum Coordinator: Nancy Tuminelly
Cover and Interior Design and Production: Mighty Media
Photo Credits: Brand X Pictures, Comstock, Corbis Images, Corel, EyeWire Images, Hemera, PhotoDisc

Library of Congress Cataloging-in-Publication Data

Doudna, Kelly, 1963-
    -Ill as in grill / Kelly Doudna.
       p. cm. -- (Word families. Set III)
    Summary: Introduces, in brief text and illustrations, the use of the letter combination "ill" in such words as "grill," "hill," "skill," and "thrill."
    ISBN 1-59197-237-X
    1. Readers (Primary) [1. Vocabulary. 2. Reading.] I. Title.

PE1119 .D675835 2003
428.1--dc21
                                                                                    2002038633

SandCastle™ books are created by a professional team of educators, reading specialists, and content developers around five essential components that include phonemic awareness, phonics, vocabulary, text comprehension, and fluency. All books are written, reviewed, and leveled for guided reading, early intervention reading, and Accelerated Reader® programs and designed for use in shared, guided, and independent reading and writing activities to support a balanced approach to literacy instruction.

Let Us Know

After reading the book, SandCastle would like you to tell us your stories about reading. What is your favorite page? Was there something hard that you needed help with? Share the ups and downs of learning to read. We want to hear from you! To get posted on the ABDO Publishing Company Web site, send us e-mail at:

sandcastle@abdopub.com

SandCastle Level: Beginning

-ill Words

fill

grill

hill

sill

skill

spill

Dad must **fill** the tank
at the gas station.

Will and his grandpa
grill hamburgers.

Tim and his family eat
a picnic on the hill.

A basket of oranges sits
on the window sill.

Lin learns the skill of origami.

The coffee spill stains
the paper.

10

Jill and Bill

12

Jill knows a boy.

His name is Bill.

Bill has a house
on top of a hill.

Bill has flowers
on his window sill.

In the summer,
Bill likes to grill.

Jill eats what Bill
cooks with skill.

Jill drinks lemonade.
She tries not to spill.

Jill has finally
had her fill.

Jill waves and says
goodbye to Bill.

The -ill Word Family

Bill	Jill
chill	kill
dill	mill
drill	sill
fill	skill
grill	spill
hill	thrill
ill	will

Glossary

Some of the words in this list may have more than one meaning. The meaning listed here reflects the way the word is used in the book.

basket a woven container, often with handles, made of wood, cane, or rushes

grill a device used outdoors for cooking food

origami the Japanese art of folding paper into shapes

picnic a meal eaten outdoors, often while sitting on the ground

sill a piece of wood that runs across the bottom of a door or window opening

tank a large container for storing or moving liquid or gas

About SandCastle™

A professional team of educators, reading specialists, and content developers created the SandCastle™ series to support young readers as they develop reading skills and strategies and increase their general knowledge. The SandCastle™ series has four levels that correspond to early literacy development in young children. The levels are provided to help teachers and parents select the appropriate books for young readers.

Emerging Readers
(no flags)

Beginning Readers
(1 flag)

Transitional Readers
(2 flags)

Fluent Readers
(3 flags)

These levels are meant only as a guide. All levels are subject to change.

To see a complete list of SandCastle™ books and other nonfiction titles from ABDO Publishing Company, visit www.abdopub.com or contact us at:

4940 Viking Drive, Edina, Minnesota 55435 • 1-800-800-1312 • fax: 1-952-831-1632